W9-AXK-744

Room on the Broom
BIG ACTIVITY BOOK

This book belongs to

....

GROSSET & DUNLAP
Published by the Penguin Group
Penguin Group (USA) LLC, 375 Hudson Street, New York, New York 10014, USA

USA | Canada | UK | Ireland | Australia | New Zealand | India | South Africa | China

penguin.com
A Penguin Random House Company

Penguin supports copyright. Copyright fuels creativity, encourages diverse voices, promotes free speech, and creates a vibrant culture. Thank you for buying an authorized edition of this book and for complying with copyright laws by not reproducing, scanning, or distributing any part of it in any form without permission. You are supporting writers and allowing Penguin to continue to publish books for every reader.

Based on the best-selling picture book *Room on the Broom* by Julia Donaldson and Axel Scheffler.

Text copyright © 2001, 2008, 2010, 2014 by Julia Donaldson. Illustrations copyright © 2001, 2008, 2010, 2014 by Axel Scheffler. All rights reserved. First printed in Great Britain in 2014 by Macmillan Children's Books. First published in the United States in 2015 by Grosset & Dunlap, a division of Penguin Young Readers Group, 345 Hudson Street, New York, New York 10014. GROSSET & DUNLAP is a trademark of Penguin Group (USA) LLC. Manufactured in China.

ISBN 978-0-448-48944-5   10 9 8 7 6 5 4 3

Room on the Broom
BIG ACTIVITY BOOK

Julia Donaldson   Axel Scheffler

Grosset & Dunlap
An Imprint of Penguin Group (USA) LLC

Sticker Jigsaw Puzzle

Use your square jigsaw stickers to complete the picture!

The witch had a cat and a hat that was black,
And long ginger hair in a braid down her back.

The Witch Has Lost Her Hat!

Can you draw it on her head and color her in?
Try designing some other hats for her to wear!

Would she suit a pirate hat?

Sticker Jigsaw Puzzles

Use your square jigsaw stickers to complete the picture.

Complete the Sticker Scene

The witch loses her hat, the bow from her hair, and her wand!
Can you find them on your sticker page and put them in the picture?

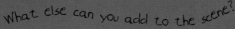
What else can you add to the scene?

Spot the Difference

Can you find ten differences between these pictures?

Color In

Can you color the picture and draw in lots of rain?

Hide-and-Seek

There are ten bows in this picture. Can you find them all?

Color In

Decorate your own bows!

Drawing and Coloring
Follow the outlines to complete each picture—then color them in!

Over the reeds and the rivers they flew.
The bird shrieked with glee and the stormy wind blew.

Find the Pair

Only two of these pictures are exactly the same. Can you spot them?

The *Room on the Broom* Album

The witch and her friends are collecting pictures for a special scrapbook.

Can you use your stickers to help them?

I love stickers!

Leaf

Wand

Bird

Owl

Flower

Fish

Frog

Bune

Buy

Dragon

Broom

Hat

Cat

Dog

Moon

Or cut out pictures from magazines!

The Broom Snapped in Two!
Use your stickers to complete the scene.

Don't forget the cat, the dog, and the frog.

Sticker Games

Look at the four patterns below. What comes next?
Use your stickers to complete them all!

Ooh, this is tricky.

Dot to Dot

Who wants to eat the witch for supper?

Join the dots to find out, then color in the picture.

Sticker Jigsaw Puzzle

Use your square jigsaw stickers to complete the picture!

It was tall, dark, and sticky, and feathered and furred.
It had four frightful heads, it had wings like a bird.

Dangerous Drawing Activity

Can you draw flames coming out of the dragon's mouth?

Go on, be brave! ~

Can You Draw a Dragon?

Use the grid to help you copy the picture, then color it in!

ASK A GROWN-UP FOR HELP

You will need:
A stick
Dry grass, straw, or smaller twigs
String or twine

🍂 Take a small bunch of dry grass
and place it around one end of your stick.

🍂 Tie the grass in place using string.

🍂 Take your scissors and snip the dry grass into
a neater broom shape.

🍂 Very soon you'll have a perfectly miniature broom,
ideal for Halloween.

Why not try hanging them up?
They make great decorations!

Make a Wand!

ASK A GROWN-UP FOR HELP

- Color in your wand, or decorate with construction paper.

- Cut carefully around the wand, following the dotted lines.

- Glue onto a thicker piece of card.

You could make your wand sparkle by adding glitter or sequins to the star at the top.

Good idea!

ASK A GROWN-UP FOR HELP

You can cast your own magic spells!

Wand Magic
Give everyone a sticker wand!

These Wands Won't Work . . .

Quick, use your stickers to place the missing stars back onto each wand.

Is There Room on the Broom?
Use your stickers to complete the picture.

Use these stickers!

Design a Broom
What a TRULY MAGNIFICENT BROOM!

Will it have seats and a shower, too?

Draw your broom here:

This broom was designed by

. . . .

Magic Stars

The witch has cast a spell! Add lots of magical star stickers around her cauldron.

Cast a Magic Spell!

Can you cast your own spell?

PoP

in

the

PoPPY

Draw the things that you
would put into a cauldron.

zoom

Iggety, ziggety, zaggety, ZOOM!

Sticker Jigsaw Puzzle

Use your square jigsaw stickers to complete the picture!

Word Search

Can you find the words in the grid below?

~~DOG~~

CAULDRON

MOUNTAIN

TREE

CASTLE

B	E	C	A	U	L	D	R	O	N
R	N	E	Y	E	G	I	T	A	P
O	T	T	R	E	E	D	V	C	B
O	U	N	V	Y	U	O	C	A	N
M	A	G	O	U	S	G	S	S	G
S	P	H	L	D	U	E	N	T	K
T	O	A	D	S	T	O	O	L	S
I	E	N	A	H	D	W	I	E	N
C	C	R	O	W	P	I	L	N	W
K	R	M	O	U	N	T	A	I	N

OWL

BROOMSTICK

TOADSTOOLS

CROW

Animal Trails

Follow the lines to find out which object each animal brings to the witch.

Who hasn't brought anything?

Drawing and Coloring
Follow the outlines to complete each picture—then color them in!

Picture Crossword

Use the picture clues to help you fill in the puzzle.

Drawing and Coloring

Is there room on the broom for a keen dog, a green bird, and a clean frog?

Why don't you draw them in and see!

It's Time for a Spooky Feast!

You could make these for a Halloween party!

Chocolate Witch's Hats

You will need:

Chocolate, ice-cream cones, chocolate cookies, sprinkles.

Ask a grown-up to melt some chocolate, and carefully spread it all over an ice-cream cone. Stick the cone to a chocolate cookie and decorate with sprinkles or sugar stars.

Star Cookies

You will need:

1 cup softened butter, 1 cup sugar, 1 teaspoon vanilla extract, 1 3/4 cups flour, icing, sprinkles.

Mix the butter, sugar, and vanilla together. Then stir in the flour to make a ball of dough. Roll it out and cut out the cookies using a star-shaped cookie cutter. Ask a grown-up to bake them in the oven at 325°F for 10 to 15 minutes. When they've cooled, decorate them with icing and sprinkles.

You could use a strip of red pepper instead of ham. ~

Frog Sandwiches

You will need:

Bread, cream cheese, ham, cucumber, grapes, raisins.

Spread a slice of bread with cream cheese and place another slice on top, then add some ham and a third slice of bread. Cut your sandwich into circles using a round cookie cutter. Give your frog some feet using triangles of cucumber, and add halved grapes and raisins to make eyes. Use a long thin strip of ham as a tongue. You could even add another raisin to make it look like your frog has caught a fly!

What truly magnificent brooms!

Cheesy Broomsticks

You will need:

Cheese slices, pretzel sticks.

Ask a grown-up to cut a cheese slice in half and make lots of small cuts along one long edge. Roll it up, and gently pull the strips apart. Now push a pretzel stick into the other end to add your broom handle.

A New Look for the Witch
Use your colored pencils to give the witch a new outfit.

You can use construction paper, too!

Star Decorations

Use the template below to create a chain of stars,
perfect for decorating your room!

🍃 Cut around the star shapes below.

🍃 Use one star as a stencil and draw
around it to make many more!

ASK A GROWN-UP FOR HELP

These would be great party decorations!

Wow!

Carefully make two small holes in each star, as shown. Thread them all together in a long line to make your decoration.

Witches in Stitches?!

Reward every good joke with a star sticker—
and every bad joke with a small, unimpressed bug.

How do you make a witch itch?
Take away her W!

RATE IT!

What do you call a witch at the beach?
A sand-witch!

RATE IT!

What is the problem with twin witches?
You never know which witch is which!

RATE IT!

Why did the witch travel on a broom?
She couldn't afford a vacuum cleaner!

RATE IT!

How does a witch tell the time?
She looks at her witch-watch!

RATE IT!

What do witches race on?
Vroomsticks!

RATE IT!

What do witches put on their hair?
Scare spray!

RATE IT!

RATE IT!

What is a witch's best class in school?
Spelling!

Face Painting!

To become the dog from Room on the Broom, *you will need:*
A sponge, a paintbrush, and face paint in brown, black, and white.

ASK A GROWN-UP FOR HELP

Dip your sponge in a little water
and paint a white background.
Add a brown circle around
one eye and on one cheek.

Outline the other eye in black and
add a nose, mouth, and eyebrows.

Finish with black whiskers.
Now you are a dog, as keen as can be!

Answers

HIDE-AND-SEEK page 13

SPOT THE DIFFERENCE page 9

STICKER GAMES page 18

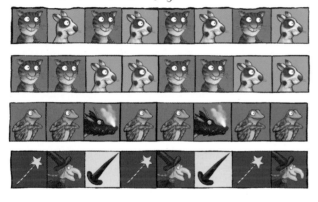

WORD SEARCH page 35

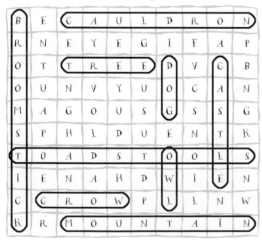

PICTURE CROSSWORD page 38

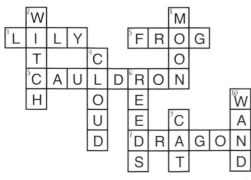

FIND THE PAIR page 12

ANIMAL TRAILS page 36

The cat brought nothing.